SA...
S0-DUT-862
Sacramento, CA 95814
08/18

WITHDRAWN
FROM COLLECTION

PROS AND CONS

THE DEBATE ABOUT THE
ELECTORAL COLLEGE

by Sue Bradford Edwards

FOCUS
READERS

www.focusreaders.com

Copyright © 2018 by Focus Readers, Lake Elmo, MN 55042. All rights reserved. No part of this book may be reproduced or utilized in any form or by any means without written permission from the publisher.

Focus Readers is distributed by North Star Editions:
sales@northstareditions.com | 888-417-0195

Produced for Focus Readers by Red Line Editorial.

Photographs ©: plherrera/iStockphoto, cover, 1; Rob Crandall/Shutterstock Images, 4–5, 11, 20–21; Harris & Ewing/Harris & Ewing Collection/Library of Congress, 7; Elena Milovzorova/ Shutterstock Images, 8–9; Red Line Editorial, 13, 31; f11photo/Shutterstock Images, 14–15; Everett Historical/Shutterstock Images, 17, 19; Alan Diaz/AP Images, 23; txking/ Shutterstock Images, 25, 44; a katz/Shutterstock Images, 26–27; Cathy Bussewitz/AP Images, 29; Joseph Sohm/Shutterstock Images, 32–33, 38–39, 45; asiseeit/iStockphoto, 35; Lo Kin-hei/Shutterstock Images, 37; Susan Schmitz/Shutterstock Images, 41; Thiago Leite/ Shutterstock Images, 42

ISBN
978-1-63517-526-4 (hardcover)
978-1-63517-598-1 (paperback)
978-1-63517-742-8 (ebook pdf)
978-1-63517-670-4 (hosted ebook)

Library of Congress Control Number: 2017948102

Printed in the United States of America
Mankato, MN
November, 2017

ABOUT THE AUTHOR

Sue Bradford Edwards writes nonfiction for children and teens. Her books include *Hidden Human Computers*, *Women in Science*, and *Women in Sports*. She and her family make a point of voting in city, state, and national elections. They discuss the issues and try to sway one another during dinner table debates.

TABLE OF CONTENTS

CHAPTER 1

UNDERSTANDING THE ELECTORAL COLLEGE

Every four years, people throughout the United States vote in the presidential election. This process is known as the popular vote. But technically, people are not voting for the president. Instead, their votes determine which **electors** will represent their state.

There are 538 electors in all. Each state has a certain number of electors. To become president, a **candidate** must receive 270 electoral votes.

Voters fill out ballots during the 2016 presidential election.

In most cases, the candidate who wins a state's popular vote earns all of that state's electoral votes. However, Maine and Nebraska are different. In these states, two electoral votes go to the candidate who wins the state's popular vote. The other electoral votes go to the person who won the popular vote in each **congressional district**.

Electors take part in a second vote. This happens one month after the presidential election. Votes from each state's electors are

➤ UPDATING NUMBERS

Throughout history, the US population has grown. The number of states has increased as well. As the country grew, the number of electoral votes also changed. In 1789, George Washington received 69 electoral votes, the highest number possible. By 1888, a candidate needed 201 votes to win. Today, a candidate must win 270 votes.

▲ Congress counts the electoral vote in 1913.

recorded on a Certificate of Vote. Certificates from all 50 states and Washington, DC, are counted in a joint session of Congress. This is when the president is officially selected.

The term *Electoral College* refers to this entire process. This process has been used to choose the president for many years. However, some people believe it is unfair. They suggest using a different method instead.

CHAPTER 2

PRO
THE ELECTORAL COLLEGE BALANCES POWER

In the United States, the federal government is the central power. State governments are the regional powers. The Electoral College helps make sure these two powers stay balanced. This balance of power is an important part of the US Constitution. **Delegates** from the states met in 1787 to create this document. They worked to create a strong central government. But they wanted states to have power, too.

In the United States, the federal government is based in Washington, DC.

Some delegates thought members of Congress should elect the president. Others wanted state governors or state legislatures to choose. Some even called for democratic elections by the people. Delegates created the Electoral College as a compromise. In this system, electors from each state vote for president and vice president.

Some delegates thought all states should have the same number of electors. However, larger states often make up a bigger part of the US economy. Plus, more people live in these states. If all states had the same number of electors, small states would have an unfair advantage.

Instead, the number of electors is based on how many members of Congress each state has. States get one elector for each member of the Senate and one elector for each member of the

▲ President George W. Bush gives a speech to both the Senate and the House in 2005.

House of Representatives. Every state has two senators. But states with higher populations have more representatives. Therefore, these states get more electoral votes. States with smaller populations have fewer electoral votes.

For example, Iowa's population is small. The state has only four representatives. Iowa gets one electoral vote for each of these representatives and two more for its senators. Therefore, Iowa has a total of six electors. In contrast, many more people live in the state of New York. This state has 27 representatives. This means New York has a total of 29 electors. Giving larger states more votes ensures they have an appropriate amount of influence.

The Electoral College also helps balance the power of the federal government with the power of the states. To win 270 electoral votes, a candidate must win votes in many states. The candidate must learn what voters in these states want or need. For instance, Hillary Clinton was the Democratic candidate in the 2016 presidential election. Clinton gave a speech in Cleveland,

Ohio. She promised to bring 376,000 jobs to the state. Candidates must address various concerns of people from around the country.

ELECTORS IN EACH STATE (2016–2020)

WASHINGTON 12	
OREGON 7	
MONTANA 3	NORTH DAKOTA 3
IDAHO 4	MINNESOTA 10
WYOMING 3	SOUTH DAKOTA 3
NEVADA 6	WISCONSIN 10
UTAH 6	NEBRASKA 5
COLORADO 9	IOWA 6
CALIFORNIA 55	KANSAS 6

CANADA

MAINE 4
VERMONT 3
NEW HAMPSHIRE 4
NEW YORK 29
MASSACHUSETTS 11
RHODE ISLAND 4
MICHIGAN 16
CONNECTICUT 7
PENNSYLVANIA 20
NEW JERSEY 14
OHIO 18
DELAWARE 3
ILLINOIS 20
INDIANA 11
WEST VIRGINIA 5
MARYLAND 10
WASHINGTON, DC 3
MISSOURI 10
KENTUCKY 8
VIRGINIA 13
TENNESSEE 11
NORTH CAROLINA 15
OKLAHOMA 7
ARKANSAS 6
SOUTH CAROLINA 9
ARIZONA 11
NEW MEXICO 5
MISSISSIPPI 6
GEORGIA 16
ALABAMA 9
PACIFIC OCEAN
ATLANTIC OCEAN
TEXAS 38
LOUISIANA 8
FLORIDA 29
ALASKA 3
MEXICO
HAWAII 4
GULF OF MEXICO

CHAPTER 3

PRO
THE ELECTORAL COLLEGE PREVENTS REGIONAL CONTROL

The Electoral College also prevents some states from having too much control. If presidential elections were based on the popular vote, states with larger populations would have more influence on the results. These states would get far more votes. For instance, California has a population of more than 39 million. In contrast, Wyoming's population is only 590,000. California has nearly 67 times as many people as Wyoming.

The Electoral College helps rural states such as Wyoming have more influence.

Therefore, California would have much more influence in a direct election.

Furthermore, candidates in a direct election would likely focus on large cities. They might ignore states where people are more spread out. But the Electoral College helps motivate candidates to **campaign** in rural states. In 2016, Maine hosted three campaign events. Nebraska had two. Mississippi held one. Without the Electoral College, rural states would be unlikely to attract as much attention.

The Electoral College gives small states the power to make their opinions heard. The 1876 election is one example. Rutherford B. Hayes ran against Samuel J. Tilden. Voters in small states supported Hayes. These states were too small to have much of an impact on the popular vote. Tilden received 264,000 more popular votes than

Rutherford B. Hayes was the 19th US president, serving from 1877 to 1881.

Hayes. But Hayes received one more electoral vote. He won the election.

Small states become especially important in close elections. In 2000, experts predicted a very close race. Every electoral vote mattered.

Democratic candidate Al Gore and Republican candidate George W. Bush worked hard to win support. Even small states were important. New Hampshire, for example, has only four electoral votes. In 2000, the state's population was approximately 1.2 million. The US population was more than 281 million. New Hampshire's residents would have little influence in a direct election. But both candidates knew it was important to win New Hampshire's electoral votes.

In addition, the Electoral College prevents one region of the country from controlling the election. For example, Grover Cleveland won large

➤ DID YOU KNOW?

In 1961, the Twenty-Third Amendment gave Washington, DC, three electors. Until then, the residents of this city could not vote in presidential elections.

Grover Cleveland used this campaign poster to gain support during the 1888 election.

majorities in six southern states in 1888. He won a total of 18 southern states, giving him the most overall votes. But Cleveland lost in the rest of the country. As a result, his opponent Benjamin Harrison received more electoral votes and won the election. Supporters of the Electoral College say it worked as designed in this election. It prevented a candidate with only regional support from winning.

CHAPTER 4

PRO
THE ELECTORAL COLLEGE
CREATES A CLEAR WINNER

The Electoral College makes it easy to determine who wins an election. In some races, no candidate wins a majority of the popular vote. This happened during the 2000 election. That year, Democratic candidate Al Gore received 50.9 million votes. Republican candidate George W. Bush received 50.4 million. Green Party candidate Ralph Nader received 2.9 million. No one received more than 50 percent of the vote.

George W. Bush became the US president in 2001 after a very close election.

Bush won 271 electoral votes. That was enough to win the election. But the popular vote was very close in Florida. Some people did not think Bush should win that state's electoral votes. The Florida Supreme Court ordered a recount of the **ballots**. As the votes were counted, Bush's lead in the state shrank. The recount dragged on until December 12. Then the US Supreme Court called for it to end. Bush was given Florida's electoral votes and was declared the winner.

Without the Electoral College, a close election might require more extensive recounts. Instead of counting the votes in only one state, people might have to recount popular votes from throughout the entire nation. This process could take much longer.

The Electoral College also helps resolve elections in which no candidate wins more than

⚠ A member of the recount group in Florida examines a ballot from the 2000 election.

half of the electoral votes. In this situation, Congress determines who will become president and vice president. The House of Representatives selects the president. Representatives vote on the three candidates who got the most electoral votes.

The Senate chooses the vice president from the two candidates with the most electoral votes.

This situation is more likely in elections with three or more **viable** candidates. For instance, no candidate won the majority in the 1824 election. Andrew Jackson won the popular vote and the electoral vote. But John Quincy Adams was a close second. Henry Clay and William Crawford came in third and fourth. Even though Jackson had gotten the most votes, the House of Representatives chose Adams to be president.

In addition, the Electoral College ensures a swift transfer of power. Electors almost always vote for their party's candidate. So, **statisticians** can often predict who will win the election before the electors vote in December. Statisticians look at popular vote totals in each state. As the votes come in, they can guess which candidate will win

National

Electoral votes (538 total)

Clinton   270 to win   Trump

218 won   14 leading   30 leading   **276** won

National popular vote

0%   50   100

▲ As the popular votes come in, statisticians can predict the election results.

that state's electoral votes. Sometimes, they can even tell who will win before voting is finished. This gives government workers more time to prepare for the new **administration**.

CHAPTER 5

CON
ELECTORS MIGHT NOT VOTE AS EXPECTED

If the Republican candidate wins the popular vote in a state, the state's Republican electors get to vote. These electors are expected to vote for the Republican candidate. If the Democratic candidate takes a state, the Democratic electors vote. They are expected to vote for the Democratic candidate. People often act as if these choices are certain. But electors do not always vote for their party's candidate.

Hillary Clinton won the popular vote in Minnesota, so the state's 10 Democratic electors got to vote.

An elector who does not vote for the party's candidate is called a faithless elector. States try to discourage faithless electors. Some states make their electors swear an oath. Other states require faithless electors to pay a fine. But many states do not have consequences. Or the consequences are not very severe. Electors sometimes ignore them.

For example, Hillary Clinton won the popular vote in Hawaii in 2016. The state's Democratic electors got to vote. In Hawaii, a law requires electors to vote for the candidate who wins the popular vote.

But one elector, David Mulinix, voted for Bernie Sanders instead. By voting for Sanders, Mulinix was protesting the Electoral College. He did not think it served people well. The Hawaii law does not discuss a penalty for faithless electors, so Mulinix was not punished.

⬆ David Mulinix believes that the Electoral College needs to change.

In Minnesota, electors must swear to vote for their party's candidate. Muhammad Abdurrahman broke his pledge in 2016. Clinton won the popular vote in Minnesota. But Abdurrahman voted for Sanders instead. Minnesota's secretary of state rejected the vote. He replaced Abdurrahman with an alternate elector, who voted for Clinton.

In 2016, four Washington electors also chose not to vote for Clinton. A Washington law fines faithless electors. The electors had to pay $1,000. This was the first time in the law's 30-year history that an elector was fined.

Several elections throughout US history have included faithless electors. So far, faithless electors have never swayed the results of an election. In each case, the same candidate would have won if all electors had voted as expected. Still, critics of the electoral process worry that one day that may change. If many electors do not vote as expected, it could be difficult to predict which candidate will win the election.

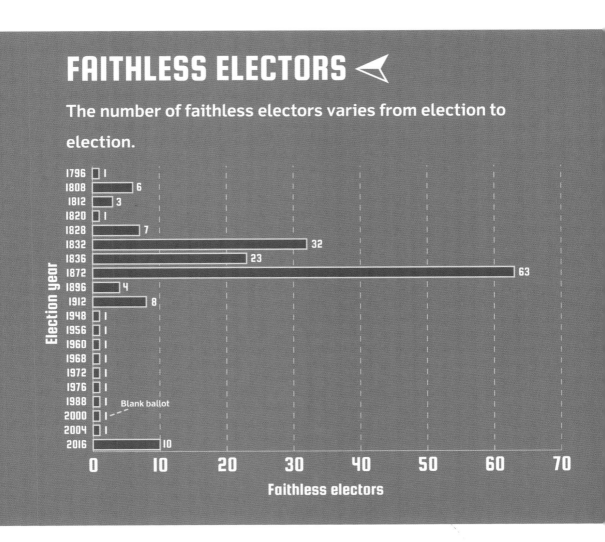

FAITHLESS ELECTORS ◄

The number of faithless electors varies from election to election.

Election year

Year	Faithless electors
1796	1
1808	6
1812	3
1820	1
1828	7
1832	32
1836	23
1872	63
1896	4
1912	8
1948	1
1956	1
1960	1
1968	1
1972	1
1976	1
1988	1
2000	1 — Blank ballot
2004	1
2016	10

Faithless electors: 0 10 20 30 40 50 60 70

CHAPTER 6

CON
THE ELECTORAL COLLEGE GIVES SOME VOTERS MORE POWER

Because of the Electoral College, some peoples' votes influence the election's results more than others. Specifically, people in large states have less of an influence than people in small states. For example, 39.25 million people live in California. This state has 55 electoral votes. That means California has one electoral vote for every 714,000 people. Only 590,000 people live in Wyoming. But the state has three electoral votes.

More than 13.2 million people in California voted in the 2012 presidential election.

As a result, Wyoming has one electoral vote for every 195,000 people. The vote of one person from Wyoming will affect the election results more than the vote of a person from California. Critics of the Electoral College say that this is not fair. Presidential candidates know that votes in some states are more influential. They will pay more attention to these voters.

The Electoral College also affects how candidates campaign. States such as California, Texas, New York, and Illinois have large populations. Therefore, they should also have a significant influence in the election. But voters in these states typically vote for one political party. For example, Texas's electoral votes went to the Republican candidate in all ten elections from 1980 to 2016. California's votes went to the Democratic candidate in the seven elections

▲ The Electoral College changes how much each person's vote is worth.

from 1992 to 2016. Candidates often assume they will win the electoral votes of states that tend to support their political party. They do not campaign as much in these states.

Instead, candidates focus on states where no political party has a clear majority. These are known as battleground states. If a candidate can change the minds of only a few hundred voters, he or she may be able to win the state's electoral votes. So, candidates work harder to address these voters' concerns. For example, Pennsylvania and Ohio are both battleground states. In 2016, Democratic candidate Hillary Clinton visited

➤ BATTLEGROUND STATES

Pennsylvania has 20 electoral votes. Ohio has 18. Candidates work hard to win votes in these battleground states. In 2008, Democratic candidate Barack Obama won the states' electoral votes. He won both states again in 2012. However, Republican candidate Donald Trump won the electoral votes from both Ohio and Pennsylvania in the 2016 election.

▲ Barack Obama campaigned in the battleground state of Ohio in 2012.

these two states more than any other state. So did Republican candidate Donald Trump. But neither candidate campaigned in Tennessee or Kentucky.

Most battleground states have medium or large populations. Candidates also tend to overlook states with the smallest populations. These states have only three or four electoral votes. Unless an election is very close, candidates focus on states with more electoral votes. Opponents of the Electoral College believe this is not fair to the American people.

CHAPTER 7

CON
THE ELECTORAL COLLEGE DOES NOT REPRESENT THE PEOPLE

In some cases, a candidate wins the popular vote but loses in the Electoral College. In the 2000 election, Al Gore led the popular vote by more than 500,000 votes. However, George W. Bush won the electoral vote. Even though more people had voted for Gore, Bush became president.

Hillary Clinton won the popular vote by an even larger **margin** in 2016. In fact, she had the third-highest total of any candidate in history.

Despite winning the popular vote in 2000, Al Gore did not become president.

Clinton received nearly three million more votes than Donald Trump. But she received only 227 electoral votes. Trump won the election with 304 electoral votes. Once again, the person who became president was not the person most voters supported.

Critics of the electoral system worry that it also fails to represent minority voters. Statistics showed that Bush led among white male voters in the 2000 election. He lost among voters who were African American or Latino. Female voters, urban voters, and people with below-average incomes did not typically vote for Bush either. Despite his narrow band of supporters, Bush won the electoral vote and became president.

Similarly, Clinton won more votes from African Americans, Asians, and Latin Americans than Trump did in 2016. But she still lost the election.

In 2016, 65.85 million people voted for Clinton, while 62.98 million people voted for Trump.

Critics say her loss proves that the Electoral College works against minorities. The election results did not reflect their opinions.

In addition, minority voters often live in cities. Cities tend to grow faster than rural areas.

In April 2010, the population of New York City was 8,175,133. By July 2016, it had increased to 8,537,673.

However, the number of electors is only updated every 10 years. As a result, minority voters are more likely to live in areas that are not represented well. States with large cities may be at a disadvantage, too.

In fact, the electoral system can make people think that their votes do not matter. This can discourage people from voting. Only 58 percent of eligible voters took part in the 2016 presidential election. In a direct election, states with high voter **turnout** would have more votes in the total. This would give them a stronger influence on the election than if fewer voters cast their ballots. More people might be encouraged to vote.

This is not the case with the Electoral College. No matter how many voters turn out, the state has a set number of electoral votes. Unless these problems are addressed, critics of the Electoral College believe the presidential elections will not represent the views of the people.

DID YOU KNOW? ◁

The last serious attempt to eliminate the Electoral College was in 1970. A bill was passed by the House of Representatives, but it failed in the Senate.

PROS

- The Electoral College motivates the federal government to consider the interests of the states.
- The Electoral College gives states proportional power.
- The Electoral College prevents one region of the country from controlling the election.
- The Electoral College helps make sure rural areas are not ignored.
- The Electoral College creates a clear winner.
- The Electoral College makes it easy to predict election results and transition between administrations.

Electoral votes (538 total)

Clinton   270 to win   Trump

218 won   14 leading   30 leading   276 won

CONS

- Some electors do not vote for their party's candidates.
- The Electoral College makes some people's votes worth more than others.
- The Electoral College causes politicians to focus on battleground states and ignore voters in other areas.
- The candidate who becomes president may not be the candidate that most people supported.
- The Electoral College does not adequately represent minority voters.
- The Electoral College can make people feel that their votes do not count and discourage them from voting.

THE ELECTORAL COLLEGE

Write your answers on a separate piece of paper.

1. Write a letter to a friend explaining how electors are chosen.

2. Do you think the Electoral College is an effective method for selecting the president? Why or why not?

3. How many electoral votes does a candidate need to win the presidential election?

    A. 227

    B. 270

    C. 304

4. Why might the Electoral College prevent one region from controlling the election?

    A. The electoral votes are spread throughout the country.

    B. The Electoral College meets in a different location every year.

    C. The electors can only vote in one presidential election.

Answer key on page 48.

GLOSSARY

administration
The group of people who work in the government's executive branch under a specific president.

ballots
Machines or slips of paper that are used to record a person's vote.

campaign
When political candidates do work, such as traveling or speaking, to convince people to vote for them.

candidate
A person running for a political position or office.

congressional district
An area that elects a member of the House of Representatives.

delegates
People who are selected to vote, act, or attend meetings on behalf of other people.

electors
People who are chosen to represent their state and vote for the president.

margin
The gap between the winner and the loser in an election.

statisticians
People who analyze information having to do with numbers.

turnout
The number of people who vote in a single election.

viable
Likely able to succeed.

TO LEARN MORE

BOOKS

Anderson, Holly Lynn. *The Presidential Election Process.* Pittsburgh: Eldorado Ink, 2016.

Heppermann, Christine. *Bush v. Gore: The Florida Recounts of the 2000 Presidential Election.* Minneapolis: Abdo Publishing, 2013.

Levinson, Cynthia, and Sanford Levinson. *Fault Lines in the Constitution: The Framers, Their Fights, and the Flaws That Affect Us Today.* Atlanta: Peachtree Publishers, 2017.

NOTE TO EDUCATORS

Visit **www.focusreaders.com** to find lesson plans, activities, links, and other resources related to this title.

INDEX

Answer Key 1. Answers will vary; **2.** Answers will vary; **3.** B; **4.** A